# DR VLOGGER

## TONY BRADMAN   WIL OVERTON

Franklin Watts
First published in Great Britain in 2018 by The Watts Publishing Group

Text copyright © Tony Bradman 2018
Illustration copyright © The Watts Publishing Group 2018

Executive Editor: Adrian Cole
Design Manager: Peter Scoulding
Cover Designer: Cathryn Gilbert
Illustrations: Wil Overton

HB ISBN 978 1 4451 5636 1
PB ISBN 978 1 4451 5637 8
Library ebook ISBN 978 1 4451 6357 4

Printed in China

MIX
Paper from
responsible sources
FSC® C104740

FSC
www.fsc.org

Franklin Watts
An imprint of
Hachette Children's Group
Part of The Watts Publishing Group
Carmelite House
50 Victoria Embankment
London EC4Y 0DZ

An Hachette UK Company
www.hachette.co.uk

www.franklinwatts.co.uk

Layla     Jayden     Caleb

They are Kid Force 3.

Layla looked at her friends. "Dr Vlogger has a big head."

"Yeah, and a big mouth," said Jayden.

"I think Kid Force 3 need to stop his evil plans."

"All right Kid Force 3. Let's go!" shouted Jayden.

"Shush!" said Layla and Caleb.

"Sorry," Jayden said quietly.

Jayden, Layla and Caleb sneaked
out of coding club. They took off.

Kid Force 3 went deeper into the base.

"He's here," said Caleb.

The screens around them came on.
Dr Vlogger appeared.

"Looking for me?" asked Dr Vlogger.

"We are here to stop your plans!"
said Jayden.

"You can't touch me. I'm not even real!"
said Dr Vlogger.

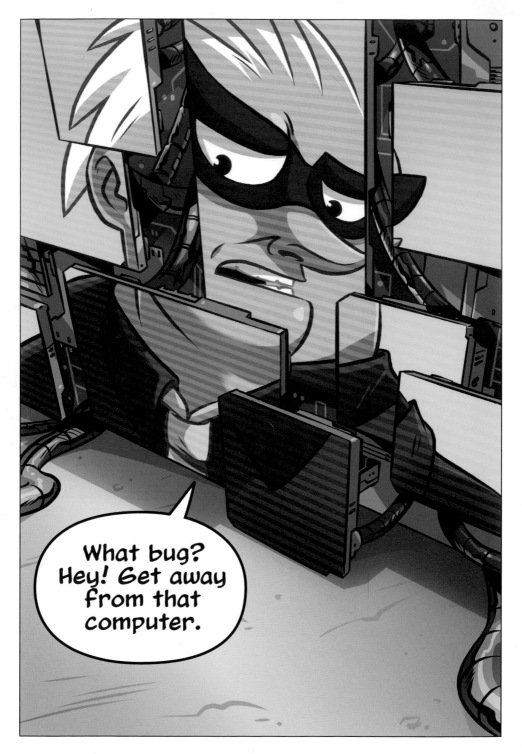

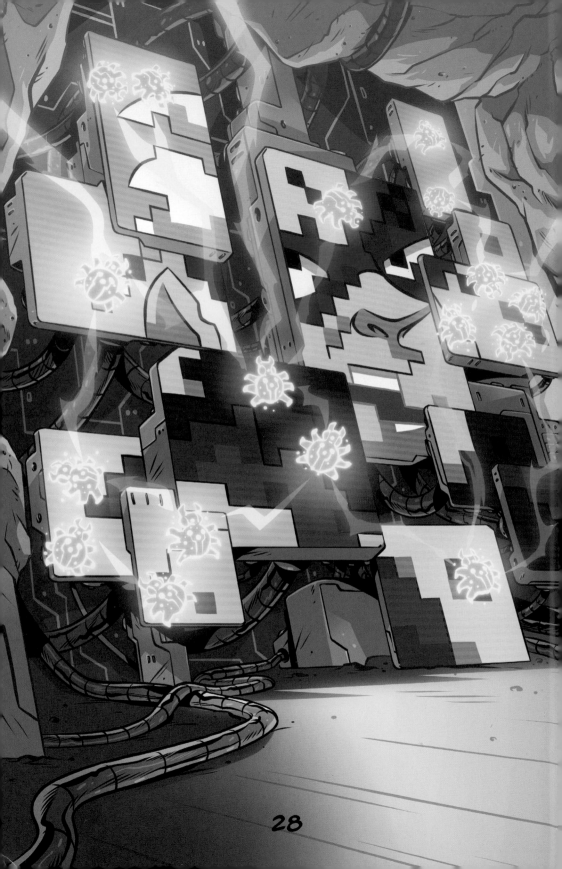

29